Flannel Kisses

Flannel Kisses

Linda Crotta Brennan
Illustrated by Mari Takabayashi

Houghton Mifflin Company
Boston

The text of this book is set in 24 point Weiss.
The illustrations are watercolor, reproduced in full color.

Library of Congress Cataloging-in-Publication Data

Brennan, Linda Crotta.
Flannel kisses / by Linda Crotta Brennan;
illustrated by Mari Takabayashi.
p. cm.
Summary: Rhyming text describes a winter day spent playing in the snow.
HC ISBN 0-395-73681-1   PA ISBN 0-618-73752-9
[1. Snow—Fiction. 2. Play—Fiction. 3. Winter—Fiction. 4. Stories in rhyme.]
I. Takabayashi, Mari, 1960– ill. II. Title.
PZ8.3.B7455F1 1997[E]—dc20 96-2997 CIP AC

HC ISBN-13: 978-0-395-73681-4
PA ISBN-13: 978-0-618-73752-9

Printed in Singapore
TWP 10 9 8 7 6 5 4 3

For my husband, who warms me with his flannel kisses.

— L.C.E.

For my husband, Kam, and our daughter, Luca.

— M.T.

Flannel sheets,
Cold floor,

Hot oatmeal,

Out the door!

Slippery snowsuit,
Sticky snow,

Pack a snowball,

Make it grow.

Pile snowballs,

Small on fat.

Crown icy head
With fuzzy hat.

Dry socks,
Soup's best.

Red nose rubs

Dad's flannel chest.

Back outside,

Dig snowy square,

Stove and table,
Hard-packed chair.

Toes cold,
Cheeks red,

Smell hot stew,

Baking bread.

Fireside story,

Say good night,

Flannel kisses
By pale starlight.